# RACE THE WILD

## SAVANNA SHOWDOWN

# RACE THE WILD

## ARE YOU READY TO RUN THE WILDEST RACE OF YOUR LIFE?

Course #1: Rain Forest Relay

Course #2: Great Reef Games

Course #3: Arctic Freeze

Course #4: Savanna Showdown

# RACE THE WILD

## SAVANNA SHOWDOWN

·BY **KRISTIN EARHART**·
·ILLUSTRATED BY **EDA KABAN**·

**SCHOLASTIC INC.**

## TO BRANT AND WILSON AND FURTHER ADVENTURES —KJE

Text copyright © 2016 by Kristin Earhart
Illustrations copyright © 2016 by Scholastic Inc.

ISBN 978-0-545-77356-0

10 9 8 7 6 5 4                    16 17 18 19 20

Printed in the U.S.A.            40
First printing 2016

Book design by Yaffa Jaskoll

# CHAPTER 1

## A DIZZYING DRIVE

I *can't believe this is happening. Again!*

Trying to fight off dizziness, Mari forced herself to close her eyes. It wasn't easy, shutting out the vast African landscape and the intense sun. The silhouette of a tree, its branches arching toward the sky, still burned in her mind.

Mari's stomach was feeling shaky, so she wrapped her right hand around her left wrist and pressed hard with her thumb. She had learned the technique only days earlier, but it had been useful. The vibration of the double-decker bus pounded in her head. The ride was bumpy, and, on the upper level, the bus seemed to sway back and forth.

She had never had motion sickness before the race, but she had also never ridden on boats in the open sea or in tiny private planes buzzing over icy mountaintops. Racing around the world for a million-dollar prize was demanding. *The Wild Life* contestants were constantly on the move, rushing to reach the next landmark and answer the next clue. All five of the remaining teams were on the bus, crammed in with tourists who were anxious to start their safaris. The teams were anxious, too.

The bus slammed to a stop and jolted the sick feeling from Mari's stomach.

"What's going on?" she asked as she stood and looked around. At once, she focused on a giraffe. It would have been hard to miss, since it was just about the tallest thing in view. Mari scanned the horizon and saw that the rest of its herd was far away, grazing across the flat grassland. She wondered why this one was on its own. Then she saw the answer: a lion. The great cat crouched on one side of the road; the giraffe stood on the other.

Mari pointed it out to her teammates.

"Oh, great," Sage muttered. "Why'd they stop? I don't want to see a bloodbath."

"What makes you think there will be one?" Mari's voice was hushed as she studied the scene.

"The lion's a top predator with piercing teeth and sharp claws on its mammoth paws. Need I say more?" Sage counted each point with a crisp flick of her fingers.

Russell and Dev, their other two teammates, remained silent as they watched the encounter.

Mari focused on the animals. The lion, a female, was crouched in the long grass. The giraffe stood tall.

"Giraffes are fast, right?" Russell whispered. "She should run for it."

In an instant, the giraffe did run, but not to escape. It charged at the lion, taking three long strides to cross the road. The lion sprang into motion. Sage flinched and looked away. But Mari wasn't surprised when the lion darted in the opposite direction.

"What?" Dev asked, his dark eyes clouded with disbelief. "What just went down?"

The bus jerked into gear again, and Mari stumbled back into her seat. It took only seconds for her motion sickness to return. But she would fight through it. She had seen a giraffe confront a lioness! She had read about how a giraffe could kill a lion with one well-placed kick. Drama on the savanna was not always predictable.

The crowded double-decker bus blazed along the dusty road through the African grasslands. It was the last leg of *The Wild Life*. The race had taken her team from the Amazon rain forest to the Great Barrier Reef to the Arctic tundra, and now to the savanna. For Mari, it had also turned three complete strangers into three of her closest friends. She didn't want the contest to be over. Win or lose, it didn't matter. She was never in it for the prize money or even bragging rights. She'd entered for the experience—and the animals. Everyone on her team knew that. When would she get to travel to such extreme locations and see so many animals in their natural habitats ever again?

Mari went back to pushing on her wrist to ward off the spinning and whirring inside her head. It was bad enough that she wasn't as athletic as her teammates—Sage and Russell were practically semi-pro as far as she was concerned—but why did she have to deal with motion sickness, too? This race was all about speed and being able to adapt to new climates and challenges. Mari felt like she was holding the others back. She might not care about winning, but they did. Sure, she knew a lot about animals, which had helped them on previous legs of the race, but she couldn't unravel the harder Wild Life clues when her brain was all fuzzy.

"Are you feeling better?" asked Sage.

Mari nodded. Even with her eyes closed, she could picture the concern in Sage's. Sage's blue eyes could be compassionate and deep like the ocean, but they also could be cold and unmoving, like an iceberg. Mari knew that the combination made her a good leader.

"Mari! You've gotta check this out!" That was Russell. He was the opposite of an iceberg— funny, loyal, and easily excited. "Look!" he called, pointing. "I've never seen a giraffe drink before!"

"Dude, we just got to the savanna. There's a lot you haven't seen before." That was Dev. The two boys were always joking around, even though they were very different. Dev knew a ton about science and tech stuff, but there was a lot more to him than that.

Mari took a deep breath and raised her head. Black dots blurred her vision as her eyes adjusted. She soon focused in on the giraffe. The bus had caught up to the rest of the herd. So cool! Mari knew that a giraffe had to spread its front legs far apart and bend down in order to get close enough to the water. The position put the animal at risk. A giraffe would never drink if there was a predator around. She hoped none of the lion's friends were nearby.

"Isn't it the middle of the dry season?" Russell asked. "Why is only one giraffe drinking? Aren't they thirsty?"

"Giraffes get almost all the water they need from the leaves they eat," Mari explained. Giraffes were fortunate. They were so tall, they could eat high leaves the other grazing animals couldn't reach. For this reason, they were less likely to go hungry.

Mari loved giraffes—with their elegant necks and graceful gait, they reminded her of her oldest sister, who ran in cross-country races. But even though the red team hadn't gotten their first clue on this leg of the race yet, she knew the giraffe would not be the answer. It was never that easy. The chances of them getting the clue while they were on the bus seemed slim. The race organizers liked to make it more of a "moment."

Still, Team Red needed to be poised and ready to answer the first clue the instant it came in. They were currently in third place, so they had a lot of catching up to do.

"I can't believe the orange team was booted, just for sending in the wrong photo," Russell said under his breath, so only members of Team Red could hear.

"I thought it was for talking with their mouths full," Dev tried to joke, but no one laughed.

"Julia from Team Purple told me they doctored the photo," Sage confided. "That's why they were kicked out of the race." Her gaze darted between her teammates and the passing stretches of dry, grassy land.

"I don't get how they could do that," Dev stated, suddenly serious. He pulled out the team ancam. The ancam was a combination walkie-talkie and camera. It was the team's sole communication device—how they received clues and submitted answers—and Dev was in charge of it. "As far as I can tell, the system is locked. There is no way to alter the photos you shoot, or to load different files. It would take an expert hack."

Mari tried to hide her smile. If Dev couldn't figure out how to tamper with the ancam and their answers, Mari doubted anyone could.

"Do you really think Bull Gordon would kick out a team just for giving a wrong answer?" Russell wondered. "It seems extreme." Bull Gordon was the host of *The Wild Life* competition. Before he became the spokesperson for the race, he had been a wilderness explorer and adventurer.

"It seems unlikely. And unfair," Sage admitted. "But we're down to the wire. Maybe it's his way of letting everyone know the competition is serious. There's no room for mistakes if you're going to win."

Russell sighed so loudly that the whole team turned to him. "I wonder what he'd do if he found out someone really cheated."

"They'd be gone in an instant," Sage replied. "And they'd deserve it."

Mari looked at Sage. The team leader had mellowed out a lot since the start of the race, but Mari suspected that Sage's old grit—her we're-in-it-to-win-it attitude—had returned.

"Well, we won't submit any bad photos," Dev reassured everyone, "just as long as Mari points me in the right direction."

"What?" Mari felt her face grow hot, and not from the burn of the sun.

"What do you mean, 'what?' You are the whiz when it comes to these clues."

"But we're a team," Mari insisted.

"Yes," Sage agreed. "And we're lucky to have you. You could have easily ended up with the other Smarties on Team Purple. You're our secret weapon."

Mari lowered her head again and stared at a rusty spot on the bus floor. She pressed harder on her wrist. Her brain ached. She didn't feel like a weapon, and she wasn't sure that's what she wanted to be.

# CREATURE FEATURE

## GiRAFFE

**SCiENTiFiC NAME:** *Giraffa camelopardalis*

**TYPE:** mammal

**RANGE:** African plains

**FOOD:** leaves, shoots, and sometimes seed pods, of a variety of bushes and trees; acacia trees are a favorite

The giraffe is the tallest land animal in the world. It also holds the record for the longest neck, even though it has the exact same number of vertebrae (bones) in its neck as humans.

Giraffes are browsers, which means they only eat from trees and bushes. During the rainy season, they can get all the water they need from leaves. During the dry season, they need to drink from a watering hole or stream once every three days. When they do, they can guzzle about ten gallons. (Open your fridge and find the biggest milk, juice, or water jug. Do the math to see just how much a giraffe drinks at one time: a lot.)

The giraffe's tongue might not hold any records, but it's still unique. It's long and prehensile, which means it's really flexible, and can wrap around things like leaves. It's also deep blue, to help protect it from the sun.

# CHAPTER 2

## SAFARI STARTUP

"**G**ood to see you all made it." The bus had come to a stop and Bull Gordon greeted them from below. The battered rim of his trademark fedora shielded his face from the sun, but his smile was still gleaming and bright.

The red team was already striding up the aisle toward the stairs. They wanted to be the first off the double-decker bus. Mari couldn't wait to be back on solid ground.

"Excuse us," one of the girls from Team Purple

said, forcing her way into the aisle right in front of Mari.

"They should let us go first, anyway, since we're ahead of them," Eliza, the Team Purple leader, insisted. "Remember, Team Red, you're in third place."

Mari's eyes narrowed. She was somewhat insulted that Sage had said she would fit in with the purple team. Sure, all the members were smart, but they weren't very nice.

Mari sighed and stepped back, letting the purple-clad contestants leave their seats.

"Hey. Us, too," a boy in lime green cut in with a chuckle. His team had been sitting on the opposite side of the aisle. "We're in the lead."

Mari glanced over her shoulder. Sage nodded. It was Russell who rolled his eyes. There was history there. Russell had known all the guys on Team Green before the race. Mari remembered that they'd played football together. It was weird, how Russell had ended up on Team Red instead of Team Green.

The four boys strutted off, each with his own swagger.

"There go your bros," Dev whispered.

"Yeah, right," Russell whispered back.

Sage nudged Mari's elbow, and Mari led her team off the bus.

"One map per team," Bull Gordon said as he placed a folded brochure in Mari's hand.

She gave him a quick smile. To her, Bull Gordon seemed like a super cool uncle or a fun science teacher.

She looked around the small rest stop, drew in a deep breath, and started feeling more like herself again.

"Two team members come with me," Bull announced. "Two stay and study the map."

Mari held up the map, and Russell moved next to her. Sage and Dev headed off with Bull. Both Mari and Russell watched as members of each remaining team joined them.

"Can you imagine being kicked out?" she said. "That would be the worst. Especially if you didn't cheat."

"It'd be worse if you did cheat," Russell replied. "Then Bull would be all, 'I'm disappointed in you. That's not how we run this race.'" Russell shook his head. "Nothing would be worse than that."

Russell was staring out at the rolling land, but he wasn't really looking at it. He turned to Mari. "You know what? There's a team that did cheat. For real. And they're still in the race."

Mari didn't have a response.

"I didn't tell anyone. It didn't feel right." Russell's face was blank for a long time. Then he shifted the weight of his hiking pack, and focused on the map. "So, where are we?" he asked, glancing around for landmarks while Mari did the unfolding.

"We're right here," Mari declared, relieved by the change of subject. There was a red star in the middle of the map, right next to a tourist rest stop. "In the middle of the Serengeti Plain. We're going to see giant herds of grazing animals.

And predators—lots of predators. It'll be amazing." Already, the possibilities churned through Mari's head. The Serengeti was the perfect place for the last leg of the race. Here they would witness wild animals being truly wild, out on the open plain. It would be a real safari.

Mari had once read that the word "safari" came from the Swahili word that means "journey." The last leg of their journey was about to begin. Mari looked up to see Sage and Dev rushing back. "We've got our clue!" Dev yelled.

"And some Jeep keys," added Sage, jangling them over her head.

As soon as the teammates were together, Dev held out the ancam so they could all crowd around and read.

This earth pig

Can really dig.

It hears its foes,

And smells its food.

Its tongue is covered

With something like glue.

# THE AFRICAN SAVANNA

**A** savanna is a large grassland that is located close to the equator. It has two seasons: winter, which is dry, and summer, which is rainy. Not enough rain falls for a forest to grow, so the gently rolling plain is dotted with bushes and a few trees. It is always warm during the day, but it can cool off at night. There are savannas in South America, Australia, and Africa.

The African savannas are home to amazing wildlife. These savannas are famous for safaris: treks through remote areas in search of impressive species. Lions, giraffes, cheetahs, cape buffalo, rhinoceroses, and many others roam these large stretches of land. The grasslands of Serengeti National Park, in the heart of Africa, boast over a million wildebeest and about 200,000 zebras.

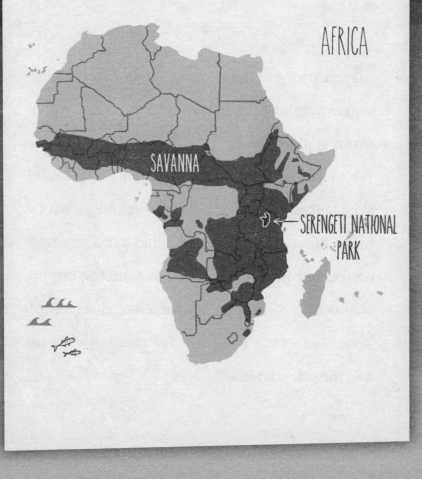

# CHAPTER 3

## BURIED DEEP

**"S**o, a sticky tongue. Maybe an anteater?" Sage suggested, keeping her voice low so the other teams couldn't hear.

"Close," Mari said, but she wouldn't offer more. She glanced around. She still didn't know what to think about what Russell had told her. She might not be as competitive as her teammates, but no way was she going to let someone cheat off of Team Red. "Let's get some distance between us and the other teams."

"Yeah, isn't that the green team leaving?" Dev pointed out. The others turned to see a Jeep filled with lime-green jerseys pull onto the dusty track. The team in first place always got to head out before the others. The second place team would go next. Team Red would be third. "How much of a head start do you think they'll get?"

"We should find Javier" was Sage's response.

Javier had been their chaperone for the first three legs of the race, and Mari was hoping that that fact hadn't changed. The teammates grabbed their gear and ran to the row of army-green Jeeps on the other side of the tourist center.

"Guys, over here!" It was Javier.

"You really dressed the part, didn't you?" Russell said, looking their guide up and down. Javier's wardrobe always hinted at their location.

Today, he wore khaki cargo shorts, a leather belt with a toolkit clip, hiking boots, and a button-down shirt with pockets. His brown-rimmed hat looked a lot like the one Bull Gordon always wore—minus the shark tooth—and the bandanna tied around his neck was bright red.

"I have hats and bandannas for all of you, too," he said, motioning to the bag on the Jeep's front

seat. "You'll need them. We're almost smack dab on top of the equator."

Russell looked uncertain, but Sage hooked the bag by its handle and handed out the accessories. Mari liked the way the hat fit snug over her thick black hair, which, as always, was pulled into a braid that fell down her back. She wondered if they'd get to keep the clothes. She felt silly for even thinking about it, but she *was* the youngest of three sisters. It would be nice to have some new things to call her own.

"Team Purple is getting ready to head out," Javier announced. "You'll be next. Do you have a plan?"

Mari could remember the first time she had seen an aardvark. It was on a nature show on TV. She had started watching wildlife documentaries when she was five, and it had become a kind of habit, like a security blanket.

As soon as they were settled in the Jeep, she gave the team the answer. "The aardvark is also called an earth pig," she explained, avoiding eye contact as usual. "But it isn't related to pigs at all. It just has a snout like a pig and can dig really well." She was relieved that her teammates no longer looked at her like she was some wildlife weirdo when she offered answers and extra facts. But she sometimes still felt like one.

After they had left the tourist center, Mari recommended they drive toward the Mara River.

"Which way is that?" Sage asked.

"Check the map," Russell suggested. "It's in the outside pocket of my backpack."

Sage stretched to reach into the back of the Jeep. After a sequence of zipping and shuffling, she sat down in her seat again.

"Got it," she announced. "So why are we headed for the river? All we need is a humble aardvark. Am I right?"

Mari noticed a strange look in her friend's eyes. "I just think we'll end up at the river at some point anyway," she answered.

"Mari, you're good. We all know that. But can you really predict what the next clues will be?"

Mari didn't want to have to explain herself to Sage. Of course she couldn't be certain, but she had watched countless nature programs on the Serengeti. If Sage had done the same, then she would also suspect that at least one clue would involve one of the most famous sights in all of nature: the epic wildebeest river crossing. Thousands upon thousands of the hooved beasts trekked over the dry plains of the Serengeti savanna, and then crossed the Mara River to reach the rain-drenched plains in Kenya. Even on Mari's small bedroom TV it looked amazing, and it happened every year at this time.

"You're right," she said with a shrug. "I can't predict it. It was just a hunch."

"But it couldn't hurt, right?" Russell said. "We could head that way while we're trying to answer the first clue."

"Sure, we can do that," Sage answered, an edge to her voice. "But we have to focus on what we know we need to find. And that's the first clue." Over her shoulder, Mari noticed Sage giving Dev a long look. Since when did Sage speak in riddles? And since when did she and Dev share knowing glances?

"So where am I going?" Javier called from the front seat.

"Toward the river," Sage replied.

"It's northwest from here," Dev added. He held the team's GPS in one hand and the map in the other.

"Everyone grab binoculars," Sage announced. "We're on aardvark watch."

Mari took a deep breath and nibbled her upper lip, noting the sun's position in the sky. "Technically, we're on aardvark-burrow watch," she said. "Aardvarks are nocturnal, so they probably won't be out for at least an hour or two, unless we're super lucky."

"What will a burrow look like?" Dev asked.

"Just a large hole in the ground, one big enough for a 100-pound animal." She lifted a pair of binoculars and began to search.

The others untangled the binocular straps and got to work, too. Javier drove on across the dry, expansive savanna at a steady pace. They wound around patches of thorny bushes and flat-topped trees, their green leaves contrasting with the golden, brittle grass. "Let me know when you want to stop," he called back to them, but no one said anything for a long time.

"I think I see one!" Dev yelled after a while. "Over there."

Mari swung around to focus her binoculars where Dev indicated. Javier pulled the Jeep to a stop. Mari soon realized, that for some reason, she was the only one looking at the potential bur-row. Everyone else was looking at her. "Okay," she said. "We should check it out."

They left their doors open and hurried over to the hole.

"I don't know if we're going to find what we're looking for here," Mari said, circling the burrow.

"It's big enough," Dev said. "I could climb down there."

"Yes, it is big enough," Mari agreed. "But there are lots of droppings scattered around. Those are too small to be an aardvark's. Something else might be living here now."

Mari hadn't expected it to be easy. She knew aardvarks constantly abandon old burrows, and new animals move in. The pig-snouted insect eaters had amazing claws, so they were expert diggers. It wasn't hard for them to build a new underground home.

"But it probably was once an aardvark burrow, so maybe there's another one around here—with an actual aardvark in it," Mari said.

"It makes more sense to look from the ground anyway," Sage said. "It was too hard to spot holes from the Jeep."

Mari knew Sage was right, but it somehow felt like the team leader was criticizing her. She noticed Russell waving her down. He was on the other side of a cluster of acacia trees, standing over something that looked at first like an old, dead tree trunk. But it wasn't that at all.

"Is this what I think it is?" he asked as soon as Mari arrived.

"Yeah. It's a good sign," she said in a near whisper. She examined the shafts of mud that rose from the ground. "If there are termites here, there's a good chance there's an aardvark as well." Mari could easily picture an aardvark lumbering up to the mound, nose to the ground. Its rounded back, long ears, and tail—thick like a kangaroo's—gave it an unmistakable silhouette. The aardvark's strong sense of smell could sniff out dinner, even when it was five feet below ground. Then, the aardvark would dig. Its sticky tongue captured the insects, and the aardvark swallowed them whole.

"I think I found another burrow," Sage called out, her voice cutting the stillness. "And I think I see a snout. Dev, get over here now!"

Dev took off in Sage's direction at once, his long legs striding through the tall grass. But, as soon as he did, a low thrum began to carry over the hot, flat terrain. It grew louder with each second. A trail of dust rose into the air and hung there. Mari lifted her binoculars and traced the dirty cloud to its source.

It was Team Green.

# CREATURE FEATURE

## AFRICAN TERMITE

**SCIENTIFIC NAME:** *Macrotermes michaelseni*

**TYPE:** insect

**RANGE:** African forests and grasslands

**FOOD:** fungus that grows on decomposing plants

Like many insects, termites live in colonies. Their society is very organized, and termites are born with one of three jobs.

Workers are responsible for building and maintaining the nest, finding food and water, and carrying it to the nest.

Soldiers protect the nest from intruders.

The queen and king make and fertilize eggs. Each colony has one of each.

To build the nest, workers create a complex system of tunnels underground. They also construct shafts that rise high above the ground—up to 30 feet. This is the part of the nest that makes up the mound. The shafts let air flow in and out and help keep the nest at an even temperature. Workers mine mud for the shafts from deep underground and stick it together with saliva.

There are species of termites that devour houses; they are destructive pests. But termites in the wild serve a purpose. The digging of African termites changes the makeup and texture of the soil, allowing different kinds of plants to grow. The termite mound can also provide a home to various animals or serve as a perch. Cheetahs in particular sit on mounds to get a better view.

# CHAPTER 4

## ON THE WRONG TRACK

"What is that sound?" Sage yelled, hands on her hips as she squinted against the sun. "It scared the aardvark away. Dev didn't even get to take a shot!"

Mari looked at Russell. She knew they were both thinking the same thing. The sound of a low, rumbling motor might frighten an aardvark, but so would the loud yell of a human being.

"Is that Team Green?" Sage asked, her tone full of disgust. Sage gave Dev a penetrating glance. "What are the chances?"

"But this is good," Russell said. "If we can see them, it means we're not far behind. We just have to get that aardvark shot."

Dev nodded, briefly making eye contact with Sage. "That's all we need to do," he agreed.

Mari had cased the aardvark burrow and found another set of holes many feet away. "We should split up, so he doesn't sneak out one of the other entrances."

"Or exits," Dev said. Mari cracked a smile. Dev had not been able to keep himself from joking during the first two legs of the race, but he'd been much quieter, more serious, lately.

"Russell, you go over there," Sage directed. "Mari, you take the far hole, and Dev and I will watch from here."

Sage's plan made sense, so Mari took her post, but before they separated, she suggested that they try to be quiet. "He won't come out if he hears us." The others nodded and went to their lookout spots. Javier left the Jeep and settled in the shade under one of the few trees. "I'll keep an eye out for other wildlife," he said. "The kind we want to avoid."

After a short while, Sage came over to Mari's spot. She kneeled down and looked out at the horizon. "So, we're assuming Team Green was heading to the next clue, right?"

"I guess so," Mari whispered. "They weren't sitting around an aardvark burrow, that's for sure."

"But how did they get a shot of a nocturnal

animal when it's not dark?" Sage wondered out loud. "Did they get super lucky?"

Mari shrugged. "Maybe." Sage had repeated the exact phrase Mari had used earlier: *super lucky*.

Sometimes aardvarks did come out during the middle of the day, but it wasn't typical. They usually waited until the sun ducked lower in the sky, and the temperature dropped lower, too.

"Is there anything we can do to lure them out?"

"Do you have some Scent of Insect spray?" Mari asked. "Anything else would probably violate the Wild Life creed. You know, the rule that says we can't mess with the natural course of things?"

Sage looked thoughtful. "Listen, Mari." Sage

paused to take a deep breath. "I want to tell you about something, but I don't want you to get upset." She paused again. Mari dropped her eyes and focused on the blade of grass in her hand. It was so dry it felt thin and fragile. "I found something in Russell's backpack. I wasn't looking for it, I swear. But I think he might be cheating."

"That's ridiculous," Mari answered right away. She looped the grass into a knot.

"I know it sounds crazy, but when he told me to get the map, I found this," Sage continued. She opened her hand. Inside was a tiny metal chip. It looked battered, like someone had stepped on it. "Dev said it's some kind of tracking device. It might explain how Team Green keeps showing up wherever we are."

"He'd never cheat," Mari said. "I know he's known those guys longer than he's known us, but that's not Russell. I know it isn't. Just ask him."

"We can't," Sage said. "Not yet. And you have to promise me you won't say anything."

Mari dragged her bottom teeth across her top lip several times before looking up at Sage. "Okay," she agreed. "I promise."

"Good," Sage said. She rested her hand on Mari's shoulder before walking away and heading back to Dev.

Mari sighed. At least she now knew why Sage and Dev were acting strange, but she had a bad feeling about that chip. She looked over to where Russell was sitting, diligently watching the aardvark hole. Mari told herself that no matter what Sage had found, Russell was on their side. And that's when he stood up and silently waved both arms back and forth, like he was directing a huge airplane.

"Dev!" Mari whispered, pointing.

Dev looked up and immediately understood. He was the only one with an ancam, after all. Stealthy like a savanna ninja, Dev tiptoed over to

Russell's side and snapped a shot. Moments later, the two boys celebrated.

"Yes!" Dev shouted, loud enough for every aardvark in a five-mile radius to hear. He and Russell marched over to the girls chanting, "Clue Number Two, Clue Number Two."

```
Splish, splash,
They are right in the path.
The strongest jaws on the planet
Stop the greatest migration on land
With one mighty, murderous
Snap!
```

"It sounds gruesome," Russell said after they had all finished reading the message. His whole face turned down in a frown.

Dev passed the ancam on, so everyone could review the clue one more time. But Mari stepped away from the group. She didn't need more hints. As soon as she had read the first line, Mari knew, *just knew*, the clue would be about the Mara River. It made sense. The Wild Life teams' visit to the savanna fell during the peak season for the wildebeest to be heading north. The scruffy-bearded, skinny-legged, hooved beasts were leaving the dusty plains of the Serengeti in search of greener pastures. It was the greatest migration on land, but they still had to cross the water of the Mara River. That was the *splish splash* at the start of the clue. And the *snap* at the end was for the crocodiles that would be waiting, ready to munch on a meal.

# CREATURE FEATURE

## WILDEBEEST

**SCIENTIFIC NAME:** *Connochaetes taurinus*

**TYPE:** mammal

**RANGE:** on open plains and acacia woodlands in Southern Africa, Tanzania, and Kenya

**FOOD:** grasses

Also called the gnu (pronounced *new* or *g-new*), the wildebeest boasts the current record for the largest mammal migration. Over 1.5 million wildebeest trek from the Serengeti plains, across the Mara River, and into Kenya each year.

The herds are almost always on the move, so calves must learn to walk within minutes of being born. They can keep up with the full-grown wildebeests when they are only a few days old. Most calves are born at the end of the herd's migration cycle, when they have returned to the Serengeti. Prime predators anxiously await the herd's arrival, instinctively knowing that there will be vulnerable young wildebeest to target.

While they resemble the cow family, wildebeest are antelopes.

# CHAPTER 5
## MIDDLE OF THE ROAD

"**Y**ou're going to say, 'I told you so.'"

"Not about this," Mari replied, but she didn't turn around to look Sage in the eye. Mari thought her team had found a rhythm, an understanding. How could Sage and Dev doubt Russell? And why wouldn't they talk to him about it? "I was pretty sure they'd ask something about the wildebeest migration," Mari admitted, forcing her other thoughts aside. "But I didn't know the answer would be the crocodile. That was a decent twist."

They were now driving toward the river, in the direction Mari had originally suggested. She sat behind Javier, next to Russell. Dev and Sage were in the back. Normally she liked the down-time between the contest tasks, but not today. There was a tightness in her chest, and it was spreading into her arms. She suddenly wanted to win *The Wild Life*. It would be the best way to prove to Sage and Dev that they were wrong.

It wasn't hard to distract herself. All she had to do was look at the landscape. It felt almost familiar. Every nature show had an episode on the great grasslands. Africa's wide, open spaces were a constant display of the predator's power. Great cats, hyenas, and jackals were designed for the hunt. But Mari knew the prey—the gazelles, zebras, and wildebeest—had their own strengths.

The two forces were always pitted against each other in a battle of dinner and death.

The Jeep didn't slow down as they passed a herd of Thomson's gazelles grazing on the flat terrain. The small antelopes with the bold black stripe across their sides looked elegant, even when snacking on grass, but Mari knew they were even more graceful when they were on the move. With their speed and bounding leaps, they were fast enough to outrun predators. And, on the open plains, they could easily spot danger.

As Team Red covered the miles, more bushes sprouted in clumps; more trees offered restful shade. "We're coming up on a visitor's center." Javier located the members of Team Red in the rearview mirror. "We should make a quick pit stop. The river isn't far ahead, and who knows where we'll head after that."

"I'm going first," Russell said as they pulled into the parking lot lined with canopy-covered picnic tables. He vaulted over the side of the Jeep and jogged to the door of the visitor's center.

"Mari?" Sage asked.

"Go ahead," Mari answered. As soon as Sage was inside the small, thatched-roof building, Mari jumped at her chance. She turned to directly face Dev. "Dev, you know there's no way Russell is cheating, right?"

"Sage told you?" Dev sounded surprised.

Mari nodded. "She showed me the chip."

"Yeah," Dev answered. "Did you see how it was smashed? I think he thinks he dismantled it, but I'm guessing it still works. Team Green probably planted it, and Russell discovered what they did but didn't want to turn them in."

This scenario made a lot more sense to Mari. "How do we know it was Team Green?"

"We don't, but they kept showing up one step behind us in the Amazon. Remember?"

"Remember what?"

Mari flinched. "Russell! You can't sneak up on people like that!" She gave him a playful shove. "Besides—"

"Your turn, Mari," Sage said as she strode toward the group. "But hurry. We're in a race. Remember?"

As Mari rushed to the visitor's center restroom, she thought how annoying it was that Sage had cut her off. They had to talk as a team. But maybe Sage was right to wait. It probably wasn't the right time while they were in the middle of the race, in the middle of a clue—and in front of Javier.

Mari told herself they'd resolve it that night. Then, when she slid the lock closed in the bathroom, she noticed something written on the top of the door.

*Eliza was here.*

It was scrawled in violet-colored marker. Eliza? The leader of Team Purple hardly came off as the graffiti-artist type, but it seemed like a tremendous coincidence. As if there wasn't enough to worry about! No matter what, it reminded Mari that they were in a race and Team Green was not their only problem. There was a good chance that Team Purple had taken back the lead. Team Red hadn't seen any sign of them since the all-girl team left the tourist center that morning. They were savvy, so Mari could only assume they'd headed toward the river, too.

Even though Mari told herself it didn't matter, she felt that tension in her chest again when she jogged back to the Jeep. It seemed to have a rhythm now, and it was tapping like a drum. She hoped it wasn't another symptom of motion sickness.

"Let's go!" she called out. She grabbed the pressure point on her wrist, just in case. She couldn't risk a bout of motion sickness now. The engine revved as Javier pulled out of the parking lot and back toward the open expanse of the Serengeti plains.

*    *    *

"You should have warned us!" Dev whirled around, overwhelmed. After about an hour of driving steadily north, the Jeep was now surrounded on all sides by wildebeests.

Mari was overwhelmed, too, yet in an entirely different way. She watched in amazement as each head of curved horns dashed past the Jeep. "I told you it was the largest land migration on the planet," Mari yelled over the pounding of hooves. "But you can't expect me to predict a stampede!" The constant rumble was punctuated by bleating calls. Mari turned south to see the rest of the herd rounding a dense growth of bushes. Beyond that, a wave of thousands more snaked over the plain. Russell stood next to her, binoculars in place.

When Javier had started to cross the wildebeests' path, there had been only a few stragglers. Then the herd had surged ahead with sudden speed. Now hundreds of the hooved animals were galloping past, churning up dust, leaping over a muddy gully, and continuing toward the river. A few small groups of zebras kept pace with the wildebeests, their strides long and even.

"How close are we?" Sage asked, her voice barely audible over the thundering hooves.

"Five minutes, tops," Javier called back. "Then we'll park and climb down for a closer look."

As soon as there was a break in the wildebeest traffic, that's just what they did.

# CREATURE FEATURE

## ANTELOPE

KUDU

THOMSON'S GAZELLE

IMPALA

**SCIENTIFIC NAME:** many different species in the family Bovidae

**TYPE:** mammal

**RANGE:** on open plains and acacia wood-lands in Southern Africa, Tanzania, and Kenya

**FOOD:** almost all are strict herbivores, eating grass, and leaves of trees and bushes; some species eat insects and small animals, which is an odd exception

Antelope is a name for a deer-like group of animals that all belong to the scientific family Bovidae. Wildebeest, gazelles, and impalas are examples of antelopes.

Antelopes are horned animals. In some species, only the males have horns, while in others, like the gazelle, both males and females have them. Antelope horns always come in pairs. Unlike deer, who shed their antlers once a antelope horns are permanent. And while deer antlers branch out like a tree, antelope horns do not. Antelope horns are made of bone covered with keratin, which is the same material in human fingernails and eagle beaks and talons.

All antelopes also have hooves that are split down the middle. Some hooves are wide to provide balance in swampy regions. Other hooves are smaller, for picking around uneven, rocky cliffs. Most African antelopes have short, hard hooves that will stand up to a long migration.

# CHAPTER 6
## CROSSING POINT

**"I**'ll come with you," Javier announced. Mari noted an urgency in his voice that she hadn't detected before. Javier often stayed behind, allowing the red team to tackle a challenge on their own, but right now he stood at the front of the group. Technically, he wasn't allowed to ~~hel~~

He was there as a chaperone ~~and~~ ~~official,~~

keeping thing~~s~~ ~~been a break in the stam-~~

~~had~~ revved the Jeep out of ~~

wildebeests' path. Now they were positioned to answer the next clue. Even though they had parked as close as possible to the river, over-grown bushes lined the high bank so the team had to weave their way to the waterway's edge.

"It's like a canyon," Mari said when she looked down. Her words got caught in her throat as she swallowed. She couldn't take her eyes off the steep drop that lead to muddy, rushing water. Despite all her nature-show viewing, she didn't understand how the wildebeest managed to reach the river, let alone cross it. Of course, many wouldn't succeed. The crocodiles had a lot to do with

"We'll h̲ for the shot here, ̲ower. I don't have an angle sees a crocodile." ̲less one of you

No one did. But they could hear splashes and goat-like calls from farther upstream. The wildebeest were near.

"I've got a rope in the Jeep," Javier said, looking back. "You could lower each other down to the riverbank."

"There," Sage said, pointing to where the ridge sloped down to a little ledge above the river. "If going down there gets us close enough, we won't have to waste time going back for the rope."

Mari wasn't so sure, but the boys fell in line behind Sage, digging the heels of their hiking boots into the dry, crumbling dirt as they slid down to the ledge. Javier went next, then reached out a hand to steady Mari.

Her three teammates inched along with impressive speed. Mari wondered if, in additi to swimming and track, Sage had competed in gymnastics. Navigating the ledge was a lot like walking a balance beam. Mari's middle sister, Eva, had done gymnastics for years, and Mari had been almost afraid to watch her on the balance beam and vault. It was scary watching someone she cared about taking a big risk. She'd usually just bury her face in a book until the end of the routine, but now she was the one doing something risky.

From the wildebeests' calls, Mari could tell her team would soon see the action. They just needed to get around this bend in the canyon. As she shuffled along, she leaned into the wall of the cliff. After a while, she spotted some stray wildebeest that had been carried by the current. With each step Mari took, there were more of them to see, until she had a view of nearly a hundred of the bearded antelopes crossing the river. They scurried down the steep bank, skirting tall patches of grass, and bounded into the swift water. Once they hit the river, they fought against the current, trying to reach the other side. As soon as one jumped into the water, another took its place and negotiated the leap.

It was a similar sight on the far bank. One would pull itself out of the river, with another right behind—a stream of wet, tired wildebeests, galloping up the steep, muddy canyon side. Once they reached flat land, they would find green grass . . . and a host of hungry predators.

Dev took the lead, ancam in one hand, searching for a crocodile. "They're hard to see," he said. "Sneaky."

Mari surveyed the waters as well. Of course, the crocs were hard to spot. That was a key to their success. By design, only their nose and eyes needed to rise out of the water, so they could float unnoticed. But on this narrow ledge, she needed to notice everything. She concentrated on her footing and did not look down unless both feet were securely planted. Mari soon realized Sage wasn't as careful.

At first, she heard the *plunk, plunk* of pebbles skipping into the water. A second later, the side of the ledge gave way and Sage dropped from sight.

"Help!" Her shriek was followed by the sound of her body skidding against the bank. But as quickly as she'd fallen, she jolted to a stop. "I caught a root," she screamed. "Help me. Please!"

Mari's heart practically stopped. If Sage fell into the river, she could become a meal for hundreds of crocodiles that hadn't eaten in months!

"I got you," Russell called to Sage. At once he was down on one knee, reaching his arm out to her while trying to keep his balance on the ledge. He grabbed Sage's wrist and steadied her until Javier got there and took her other hand. They dragged her up together.

"We should have used the rope," Javier concluded. "Better to waste time than one of your lives."

"What are you talking about?" Dev asked. "I didn't waste any time catching that croc." When he turned back to them, he sported a big smile. He waved the ancam back and forth. Mari glanced

down at the screen and saw the dark back of a wildebeest wrapped around a crocodile's jaws. When she looked over Dev's shoulder, she saw the same croc in the river. It opened its mouth wide to adjust its bite.

The ancam made a familiar whirring sound as it processed the photo.

"Dev, that's great," Sage said, still on her knees and trying to catch her breath. Her face was smeared with sweat and dust.

"Now let's get back up the ridge," Javier directed. "Carefully." He took the anchor position and pointed out which path he thought was best.

Mari's heart was pounding. She had just witnessed one of the greatest events in all of nature! On top of that, one of her friends had nearly become a crocodile snack, and another had saved her from that fate. Mari was certain Sage could no longer question Russell's loyalty. She hoped they could get back to being a unified team and that now everything would be all right.

But when they returned to the Jeep, she realized that everything was not all right. It was all wrong.

# CREATURE FEATURE

## NILE CROCODILE

**SCIENTIFIC NAME:** *Crocodylus niloticus*

**TYPE:** reptile

**RANGE:** Eastern and Southern Africa

**FOOD:** birds, amphibians, turtles, antelopes, zebras, rodents, gazelles, waterfowl, hyenas, cheetah, and any other animal it can clamp between its jaws

The crocodile has the most powerful jaws in nature. With an extra-wide bite and extra-sharp teeth it can catch extra-large prey, up to two times its own weight. The crocodile also has special sensory bumps on its head and body that are over three times more sensitive to touch than human fingertips. There are a tremendous number of the bumps around the mouth, so they might help the crocodile know when—and what—to chomp.

Short, powerful legs and webbed feet make it a sleek and speedy hunter in the water. Crocodiles are not quite as quick on land, so they usually wait to ambush prey as it arrives at a watering hole for a much-needed drink.

Africa is home to four species of crocodile. The Nile crocodile is its largest, and the second largest in the world.

# CHAPTER 7

## DARKNESS
## REVEALS

"**W**ho went through our stuff?"

Mari voiced the question, but everyone was wondering about the answer. Clothes, reference materials, and wrapped snacks littered the ground around the Jeep. All of their bags were empty, even Javier's.

Russell immediately plunged his hand into the outside pocket of his backpack, digging around. His eyes were frantic when they met Mari's.

"That makes zero sense," Javier said. "Why would anyone waste time ransacking our supplies?"

Mari could guess why. She assumed her teammates could as well. It had to be the green team, searching for the chip they'd planted back in the Amazon rain forest. If Russell turned it in to race officials, he could get Team Green kicked out of *The Wild Life*. It was as easy as that. And if they explained it to Javier now, all of Russell's friends, kids who lived in his town and went to his school, would be disqualified.

"Come on," Javier said. "You can think about the clue while we pick up this mess. Dev, give it to us."

With all the excitement, they had forgotten to read the next clue. Mari took a deep breath, hoping all those nature programs would come through with the information her team needed.

> Silent spots,
> Stealth paws,
> The shadow's great ghost
> Stalks the night alone.

It was a freebie! Mari couldn't believe that a clue at this stage would be so easy. It was short, but there were lots of hints.

When she heard "spots," she immediately thought of the cheetah and the leopard. The word "stealth" indicated that it was a predator, and "paws" hinted the answer was a species of cat, dog, or hyena. But the biggest giveaways were "great" and "night." They eliminated the cheetah altogether. The cheetah was not a great cat, and it hunted during the morning and afternoon.

When Mari tuned in to her teammates again, they were still eliminating answers.

"What about the hyena?" Russell suggested.

"Hyenas do their best hunting in teams," Mari chimed in. "The leopard is solitary. It lives and hunts alone. That's our answer."

"Well, okay then," Javier said with a decisive nod. "And where will we find our leopard?"

While figuring out the answer had been easy, Mari didn't think finding an actual leopard would be. As the clue hinted, the leopard was so sneaky, so stealthy, it was like the ghost of a shadow.

"They like trees, so maybe we can find one around here," Mari suggested, but the daylight was growing thin. They couldn't afford to waste time—and gas—driving aimlessly around the savanna.

"Hey, wait," Dev said. "There's another clue!"

```
Fire from above,
Fire from within,
Walls that imprison
And protect.
A habitat, a hole.
Nearly perfect,
Or nearly wrecked?
```

"Mari?" Russell asked, his voice uncertain. "What do we do with that?"

Mari could feel her teammates' eyes on her as she pondered the clue. "I'm not sure," she said, stuffing a sweatshirt in her backpack. "But I think it's giving us our next destination. Where's the map?"

"I've got it." Sage unbuttoned her cargo shorts and pulled out the map Bull Gordon had given them earlier that day. When she placed it in Mari's hand, something fell to the ground.

"How did you get that?" Russell asked. The tiny piece of metal reflected the fading light. Russell's eyes flashed to Sage as he bent down.

Out of the corner of her eye, Mari saw Sage lunge forward. Without thinking, Mari scooped up the chip and closed it in her hand.

"We can talk about it later," she said, avoiding the surprised gazes of her teammates. "Let's figure out where we're going."

Mari could feel Sage's hesitation. "Fine. Go ahead," their leader said.

"What are you thinking, Mari?" Dev did his best to sound upbeat and get the team back on track.

Mari tried to focus. "Millions of years ago, this part of Africa was covered in volcanoes, and they erupted," she explained, her finger tracing over the map.

"So that must be the fire within," Dev quickly surmised. "Magma."

Russell took a step closer to see the map better. "And maybe the sun is the fire above? Because it's so strong here?" he offered.

"Probably," Mari said.

"But what are the walls that imprison and protect?" Sage asked, moving on. "That's the key."

"My guess is it's a crater, a volcano that essentially collapsed on itself. If I remember correctly, the largest crater in the world is at the southern end of the Serengeti." Mari paused, her finger now resting on one spot. "Lots of species live there. They're kind of trapped inside its walls."

"Sounds like that's probably it," Sage agreed.

"It's called the Ngorongoro Crater." Mari hoped that was enough info for now. She didn't feel like giving a full lecture.

Her other three teammates leaned in to locate the Ngorongoro Conservation Area.

"Head south, southeast," Dev called out.

"Got it," Javier answered. Everyone piled into the Jeep. The engine revved as the Jeep pulled onto the dirt road.

Sage flopped back in her seat. "How do you know all these things?" she asked, her voice tinged with disbelief.

Mari stared out of the Jeep. Twilight had settled on the savanna. A family of elephants were silhouetted against the pink and orange sky. It was so beautiful, it hardly seemed real. This was the last leg of the race. It was almost over. She guessed it wouldn't be so bad if everyone knew.

"I had to have surgery when I was six. It was a pretty big deal, and I was in bed for weeks. My older sisters were nice about it, but they were busy with sports and friends. It's not like their lives had to stop, too, so I watched a lot of TV." Mari hesitated, gazing as the sun's golden rays burst from behind an indigo cloud. When she was recovering, the flash and color of cartoons had annoyed her. She'd been weak, and almost everything wore her out. There was only one thing she could tolerate. "I watched every nature show I could find. Over and over. And over. Even when I was better, my sisters gave me nature books for Christmas and stuff like that. I guess they thought it was my thing."

"It's your thing, all right," Russell said. He turned to look out the other side of the Jeep.

Dev had been typing *Ngorongoro* into the ancam. "That was it," he announced a moment later. "The organizers sent the GPS coordinates for the crater. Way to go, Mari. Now we just need to spot the leopard, no pun intended." Dev gave Mari's arm an encouraging punch as he pushed his way between the seats to the front, where he sat down next to Javier. The two talked for a while, then everyone went silent.

Mari's thoughts were still with her sisters. They had been the ones who sent in her Wild Life application. They had told her she should compete. They had that kind of courage. Sometimes Mari wondered how she was even related to them. But they had convinced her she could do it. Like with so many things, Mari had taken their word for it. She had almost believed them, until now.

Now she had a contraband tracking system in her pocket, a team of near strangers who had lost their bond, and a feeling in her gut that she didn't understand.

# SPOTTING A CHEETAH OR LEOPARD

The cheetah and leopard both have spots, but only one of them—the leopard—is one of the great cats, like lions and tigers. There are easier ways to tell these two successful predators apart. Here are some of them:

CHEETAH

# LEOPARD

A cheetah's spots are round or oval. A leopard's are shaped like a flower with a dot in the center.

Leopards are nocturnal (active at night), while cheetahs are diurnal (active during the day).

Cheetahs can run up to 70 miles per hour. Their speed is the key to their hunting strategy. Leopards stalk their prey and pounce on them.

Leopards, like most cats, have fully retractable claws, which means they can pull them into their paws. These are helpful in climbing trees. Cheetahs' claws are short and semi-retractable, so they act like cleats and give cheetahs traction when running.

To allow for better breathing during a fast chase, the cheetah's skull has extra space behind its nose. The leopard's does not. Instead, its skull has extra-strong jaws that can crush the bones of its prey.

Cheetahs look like long, lean track stars. Leopards are stout and muscular like football players.

# CHAPTER 8

## A SLiP OF THE CHiP

It was way past midnight when they arrived at their checkpoint. Mari couldn't believe they'd seen a leopard devouring a gazelle in the high bough of a tree on their long nighttime drive. Afterward, the teammates had eventually fallen asleep and were now puffy-eyed and bleary-brained. The sighting felt like it could have been a dream. *A somewhat disgusting dream*, Mari thought. But it was the answer to the clue just the same.

She swung her backpack on and stumbled out of the Jeep. Mari had expected a tent or a hut, but this place made her feel like she was still dreaming. Warm, welcoming torches glowed on either side of an impressive, carved wooden door. The roof appeared to be made of braided grass. Multiple turrets with circular windows gave the building a rustic—and showy—charm.

Mari felt out of place. The checkpoint seemed too luxurious to fit into the rugged landscape. And among all the confident, adventurous contestants in the race, she felt . . . she didn't know how she felt. Digging her hands into her pockets, she found something that made her even more uncomfortable: the tracking chip.

A golden light escaped as the magnificent door opened. Mari recognized the tall frame of

Bull Gordon. Javier quickly strode to greet the head of the competition. At once, the two seemed deep in conversation. Bull motioned to something past the parking area, and Javier nodded.

"Come on, Mari," Russell said as he hopped out of the Jeep and headed for the big wooden door. Sage and Dev were close behind.

"Coming," Mari said. "Just making sure I have everything." She lowered the floor mat, slammed the door, and joined her team.

"Red Team," Javier said, tapping each one on the shoulder as they passed. "Check in and then get some sleep. You will be up early tomorrow."

The next morning, Mari was roused from a fitful sleep by a knock on the girls' bedroom door.

Sage, who was already fully dressed, opened it.

"What did you do?"

"Good morning to you, too, Russell." Sage rolled her eyes. "You too, Dev."

"Seriously. What did you do?" Russell asked again, his tone almost threatening.

"I got up and took a shower," Sage replied. "It felt really good. The bathroom here is pretty fabulous."

Mari was suddenly awake, fully aware of what the day would bring. "What's going on?" she asked, scrambling out of bed.

"I don't know, but something happened with Team Green," Russell said. "It sounds like they got some kind of penalty. And I'll bet they're going to blame it on me."

The look on Russell's face was just what Mari had hoped to avoid when she had made her decision the night before. "I don't get it," she said. "You didn't do anything."

"That's what I said," Dev insisted. "But Russell isn't thinking logically."

Sage and Mari stepped away from the door so their teammates could come in. "Eliza from Team Purple said that Bull and some of the chaperones heard there were poachers nearby last night, so they went to investigate. And Team Green followed them," Dev explained.

"Poachers?" Mari questioned. Stories of people killing animals for their tusks or fur or horns had always upset Mari. Now that she'd actually seen many of the animals in the wild, it was even harder to believe that anyone would do something so cruel. "Team Green isn't interested in poachers," Mari said with certainty. "They only care about winning this race." It was too early to piece so much information together, but she was starting to get an inkling of what might have happened.

"It's my fault," she concluded. "I was the last one with the chip, and I purposely hid it in the Jeep."

"Why'd you do that?" Russell inquired, his forehead etched with confusion.

"Yeah, why?" Sage repeated.

"Because I didn't like what it did to our team. Sage, you suspected Russell, but you wouldn't even talk to him. It wasn't fair." Mari felt the urge to examine her fingernails or tug at her braid, but

she forced herself to look each of her teammates in the eye. "And Russell, you never told us about the chip. You found it all the way back in the Amazon, didn't you?" Mari remembered how she and Russell had hidden in the massive roots of the kapok tree on the race's first leg. The green team had come so close to finding them. They must have followed them using the chip, even then.

"Yeah," Russell admitted. "I found it on my backpack and didn't really know what to do."

"Dude, you should have told us," Dev said. "I would have noticed that thing was still active."

"I probably should have, but those guys were my friends." He turned to Mari.

"So all you did was leave the chip in the Jeep?"

"That's all I did," Mari confirmed. "The chaperones must have taken the Jeep out to look for the poachers."

"If the green team hadn't been tracking the chip," Dev added, "they never would have gone out last night."

"That's why they got a penalty," Mari added. She put a hand on Russell's shoulder. "So, as I see it, those guys who were your friends can't blame you at all."

"Mari, that was pure and utter genius!" Sage declared. She raised her hand for a high five.

"I didn't do it to trick them," Mari confessed, her hand still at her side.

"I know you didn't." Sage's tone turned serious as she dropped her arm. "Russell, I'm sorry I suspected you. I just was looking for a reason why we weren't in the lead."

"We weren't the fastest." Russell summed it up. "That's why we aren't in the lead."

"Then today, that's what we'll have to be," Mari said. She walked to an oversized window that looked out over the crater. The crater was enormous, large enough to be its own ecosystem. Soon, they would learn what their challenge would be. "We have to be the fastest to win."

As soon as she said it, a knock sounded on the door, and an envelope slipped under it.

# SURVIVAL OF THE SAVANNA

The African savanna is an ancient ecosystem. All life is connected in a delicate balance.

But some things threaten that balance. Large herds, like zebras, wildebeests, and gazelles, require lots of space. They need huge stretches of grassland to migrate. When humans intrude on that space—building roads or homes—they interfere with the animals' needs.

Another problem the savanna faces is

poaching, which is the illegal killing of animals. People will pay for meat, furs, tusks, and horns. They want them for a variety of reasons: for food, as trophies, or because certain animal parts are thought to have sacred healing powers. This trade puts some of the world's most endangered animals at greater risk. Wildlife organizations are working to combat this problem. Some animals or herds have guards, protecting them around the clock.

The animals of the savanna are an amazing resource. Tourism brings money and attention to wildlife and the areas where the animals live. When people come to see animals in their natural habitat, it proves that live animals are valuable. But tourism encourages development of modern communities in wild spaces. Finding a healthy balance for humans and animals may be the greatest challenge of all.

# CHAPTER 9

## A VIEW FROM ABOVE

**"Y**ou never said anything about being afraid of heights before," Russell said. He knelt close to Mari, who sat cross-legged on the ground, looking out over the expanse of the crater.

So far, Mari had been able to deal with her fear of heights, but a hot air balloon ride over a gigantic crater sounded like extended torture. She'd opt for a zip line—or even the ledge over the Mara River—four more times, rather than having to do this.

But that wasn't an option. Today the race would come to an end. After Team Green was penalized for their late-night outing, Team Red had moved into second place behind Team Purple. Now all of the teams were set to take off in hot air balloons. They'd have to answer a final clue while crossing over the crater, land on the other side, and sprint to the finish line. Then the race would be over.

"Don't worry, Mari," Dev said, "hot air balloons are totally safe."

"That's all you're going to say? You always have super-scientific explanations, but now you're going with 'totally safe'?"

"We're kind of in a hurry, seeing as we're supposed to take off in, like, three minutes," Dev said, checking the time on the ancam. "I didn't think you wanted the comprehensive 'propane burner heats the air, hot air expands, creating upthrust, lifting the basket in the air' explanation."

"Point taken," Mari said, still gazing down into the crater. It was hard to believe so many of the animals she'd dreamed about lived together right below her.

"What's the deal, Mari?" Now Sage had joined them. Her hiking-boot-clad feet came to rest squarely in front of Mari's bent knees.

"I'm just working up my nerve," Mari answered.

"No," Sage replied. "You've had nerve this whole race, whether you realized it or not. We wouldn't be here without you. What happened to 'we have to be the fastest to win'?"

"That was before I realized we'd be floating a billion feet in the air," Mari argued.

"So what? This is your chance, Mari," Sage demanded in a tone that was half cheerleader, half tyrant. "You deserve to win this, and I know you want to."

When Mari looked up at Sage, she felt it again. That burning in her gut. She hadn't known what it was before, but she did now.

"You're sure you have the instructions?" Mari checked with Dev one last time.

"I told you, they're on the ancam," Dev assured her. "We're set. And it's not like I'm actually flying the thing. We have a professional pilot." Dev motioned to a woman in a khaki vest and sunglasses who was already in position at the burners. "We just have to give her the directions."

The four teammates joined the pilot, packing themselves into the large wicker basket that was attached to the red-checked balloon. Not far away, a purple-striped balloon lifted into the sky. In the other direction, balloons of green, yellow, and blue lined the crater's rim.

Mari glanced at Russell. The teams had been separated ever since the envelopes went out that morning. No one on Team Red had spoken to anyone on Team Green.

"You'll get the last clue after you're in the air," Javier instructed them. "You need to send your answer before you touch down on the other side."

"We've got this," Mari said to their chaperone. She was surprised by the certainty in her voice.

"Twenty seconds," an organizer with a stopwatch announced from behind Javier. Dev took his place by the burners, ready to tell the operator to crank up the flame.

Ten, nine, eight, seven . . .

Mari gripped the edge of the basket.

. . . six, five, four, three . . .

Mari closed her eyes and took a deep breath.

. . . two, one, GO!

Javier helped the race organizers untie the balloon from its anchors. Mari felt the basket lift off the ground. She opened her eyes to find the balloon hovering over the crater's lip, just above the plants that blanketed the descending walls in green.

Soon they floated over a small forest, and the team grabbed their binoculars to search for the baboons, monkeys, and elephants that took refuge in the leaves.

"What? There's a lake in here, too?" Sage cried. "This place is unreal."

"There's actually a year-round freshwater source," Mari explained. "It's the only way the crater can support so much life."

Hippos hogged the swampy side of the crater floor. Snuggled in between lush aquatic plants, they stayed mostly underwater. It was the best way to protect their skin from the sun's strong rays.

When Mari looked beyond the crater walls, she could see small villages of rectangular huts. She remembered reading about the Maasai warriors, who raise cattle in the plains just beyond the crater. But for her, the real draw was inside the inactive volcano.

"I don't get it," Sage said after a while. "Why did the clue say that this place was 'almost perfect, or almost wrecked'?"

"I don't know," Mari admitted. "Maybe it's because the crater is closed off. Most of the animals are trapped in here, so there isn't a lot of new blood to keep the species healthy." Mari knew that could be an issue, but, as far as she could see, it appeared to be a vital, dynamic ecosystem.

"The wind direction is just right," Dev said, gazing at the open sky. "It should guide us straight over the crater." Every few minutes, he instructed the balloon operator to turn on the burners to steady the balloon's height. "The ancam's buzzing," he announced soon after they had passed the swamp. He reached into his pocket and then read the clue.

Part 1: Take a picture of four
different species.
Do not repeat answers.

"What?" Russell asked. "That's the big clue?"

"That's what it says," Sage confirmed, reading over Dev's shoulder. "That's weird."

"Well, you've got your pick," said Dev, motioning

with his free hand. "There are flamingos, buffa-los, hippos."

Despite being hundreds of feet in the air, Mari felt let down. This was the final challenge? Take a bunch of pictures? She knew *The Wild Life* was just a race, but she had convinced herself she wanted to win. But if it came down to speed instead of knowledge, she wouldn't be much help to her friends. She had never been fast.

"We should each take one, right?" Sage suggested.

"Well, yeah," Russell said with a shrug. "Being a team and all."

"I'll go first," Sage offered in typical leader mode.

They were now flying over the stretch of plains. Sage took a shot of a lion pride, basking in the sun. She handed the ancam to Russell, who scanned the crater floor. "Zebras," he declared. "They're cool." He checked the screen and then offered the ancam to Mari.

"Give it to Dev," she said. "I'll go last."

Russell tossed it to Dev.

"Be careful!" Mari begged. "We need that."

Dev caught the device and looked around. "I'll go with the hyenas, because they love a good joke."

Mari smiled as he took the photo. "You know they're not really laughing, right? That's just how they communicate."

"Yeah, sure," Dev said, handing the ancam to Mari. "I knew that."

"And hyenas get a bad rap for being scavengers, but most predators will steal an easy meal if they can get it."

"Good to know," Dev replied.

Mari looked down into the crater. She was ready. She had been holding out, but the balloon was directly above a group of black rhinoceros now. She wanted the majestic, endangered mammal to be her shot. She had to lean over the basket edge to get a rhino in the frame. Just as the ancam focused on a rhino's weathered face and crusted horn, Mari slipped. She tried to catch herself, but realized that it was actually the tiny device that was falling. "No!" she yelled and threw her hands out. She lurched forward and her body tipped over the basket's edge. Her fingers fumbled around the ancam, just as three sets of arms latched around her.

"I got it! Pull me up," Mari called. Her teammates tugged together, and Mari collapsed on the basket floor.

"That was crazy," Russell exclaimed. "What were you thinking?"

"We can't win without the ancam," Mari stated.

"Um, we can't win without *you*," Sage insisted. "But since we have you, I need to ask if you got the shot?"

Mari turned the ancam over in her hand and pressed the VIEW button. A blurry shot of short grass appeared. "No, I'll try again." She stood up and framed the photo, but something was wrong. "It's jammed. It won't take."

Dev, who knew the device best, examined it. "Mari's right, as usual. We only have pics of the lion, hyena, zebra, and some grass. And it won't take another."

"We can't delete or anything?" Sage asked.

Dev shook his head.

"We should complain," declared the team leader. "It's not fair that their technology failed us."

Mari's stomach clenched.

"Do we have to?" Russell wondered out loud. "Grass is a living thing. It's a species that lives in the crater."

Mari had been so disappointed about the black rhino that she hadn't thought of that. "He has a point. The clue just says 'species,' right?"

"We're nearing the edge of the crater," Dev pointed out. "And we're about even with Team Purple. What should I do?" They had passed over Ngorongoro's floor, and the flat plains had been replaced by the lush bushes and trees that grew up the side of the sloped crater wall. The race was almost over.

Sage looked around the group. "Do we agree?"

Mari and Russell looked at each other and nodded. But what if Bull Gordon and the organizers were strict about the last clue? At least the red team was together on this.

"Go ahead," Sage instructed. "Submit the pictures."

Dev punched the button and waited.

"So," Sage prompted.

"Nothing," Dev replied.

Sage eyed the purple-striped balloon. "Can't we make this thing go faster? I mean, they're right there. We've almost caught up."

"Not really," Dev admitted as he glanced at the balloon operator. "It pretty much goes with the wind. Once we're over the crater, we'll cut the burners and pull this cord. It'll let the air out so we can land. Then we'll run for it."

Sage began to rock back and forth from one foot to the other. "I didn't think we had a chance, but now I think we do."

Mari bit her lower lip. Russell seemed to shrug with his eyebrows. "Either we win or we don't," he said. "No big deal."

Sage didn't say anything; she just scowled.

# NGORONGORO CRATER

Ngorongoro is an extinct caldera volcano. Extinct means it is no longer active and will not erupt. A caldera is a specific type of volcano where the center collapses after an eruption, leaving a sunken pit with high walls. Ngorongoro is the world's largest unbroken crater that is not filled with water. It measures about 11 miles across for a total of 102 square miles. That's about the size of Orlando, Florida. Ngorongoro is 2,000 feet deep.

As if that isn't amazing enough, there are more species living in the crater than in any other space that size. The walls are dense with lush trees, a perfect hideout for leopards. There are swamps for hippos, flamingo-filled lakes, and stretches of grassland that host cheetahs, lions, zebras, elephants, gazelles, buffalos, and more. The Maasai, one of the local tribes, also graze their cattle in the crater.

While many of the birds migrate, including the famous flamingos, most of the animals live there year-round. For some species, the lack of

new bloodlines can be unhealthy. Recently, the crater has been home to over sixty lions, but drought and disease cause their numbers to fluctuate. In the late 1960s, illness took the lion total from over 75 down to 12.

# CHAPTER 10

## A WILD RACE

As the balloon rose to the top of the crater, they all could see it: *The Wild Life* banner lit by the midmorning sun. Bull Gordon stood at its base. It wasn't very far, about the distance of a relay sprint. There was a line on the ground that marked the finish, the end. "We all have to cross," Sage said. "It doesn't count until the whole team is on the other side of that line."

"Burners are off," Dev said as the operator yanked a cord. "Get ready to land!"

Mari spotted Team Purple touching down. Team Red hit the ground right after. They all scrambled out of the baskets, flag in sight. Taking deep breaths and long strides, the quickest team members crossed the line.

Mari ran as fast as she could. She didn't want to let her friends down. She watched as Sage, then Russell, then Dev crossed the finish line. But three of Team Purple's members were right there with them. Only Mari and the last girl from the purple team were still running. They crossed the line neck and neck. It seemed they had tied.

"What do we do now? Team Purple should win," Eliza demanded. "We were in first place going into the last challenge."

"That's true," Bull Gordon said, tapping the scar on his chin. "But we are not done yet.

Remember, you've only completed part one of the last clue. It's time for part two." He paused and let the contestants gather their thoughts. "Now locate your ancams and review your four photos. The team who explains how all four species are connected and types in their answer first will win."

The next thing Mari knew, Dev had placed the device in her hand.

"I can't type fast," she claimed. "Someone do it for me."

Russell snatched the ancam away. "Go," he prompted.

Mari bit her lip.

"Fast, Mari," Sage reminded.

"So, the hyena hunts lion cubs and lions

stalk the zebras that graze on the grass," Mari said. "There are lots of other ways, but that's the—"

Russell had turned away. Dev and Sage had already given their nods of approval, and their ancam had landed in Bull Gordon's open hand.

When Russell returned to the group, Mari looked at him with admiration. "Video games," he said, wiggling his thumbs.

Meanwhile, Javier and a number of clipboard-carrying race organizers were huddled around Bull Gordon, who held his arm out at full length so they all could see the answer on the screen.

Eliza scurried forward and forced Team Purple's ancam into Bull's other hand. As the race host tucked both devices in his pocket,

Mari saw a sly smile tug at the corner of Javier's mouth.

Her chest went tight, and Bull Gordon stepped forward.

"Congratulations to the winners of *The Wild Life*, Team Red," Bull Gordon announced.

The rest of the team exploded. Mari stood still, amazed.

It was a race, and they had won it. She had done her part.

Javier rushed up and simultaneously hugged them all. "I really hoped you'd win," he admitted, his usually mellow demeanor replaced with glee. "You guys had a lot going for you."

Next, Bull Gordon approached the happy four. "Rather ingenious, including a plant as one of

your four photos," he stated. "That makes the connection of all the species much easier, looping in your grazing herbivores like that."

"It was all Mari," Sage said, placing a hand on Mari's shoulder and pulling her close. "She is a real wildlife genius."

"But it took all of us to win," Mari objected. "It took the whole team."

"Yes," Bull agreed, looking her in the eye. "It always does."

The boys were too excited to have really heard her. They were in their own tiny huddle, chanting, "A million dollars, a million dollars!" The other hot air balloons were starting to land, and the contestants all wanted to hear about the final showdown.

The guys from Team Green rushed to congratulate Russell, as if they would always be the best of friends. Eliza had cornered Sage by the refreshment table, and Mari could only imagine where that conversation was headed.

While she had her chance, Mari made her way back to the rim of the crater. The tight feeling in her chest seemed to be gone, and she wasn't sure anything had replaced it. She raised her binoculars and took in the sights, without a clue or a finish line to worry about. Following the rising of the sun, Jeeps had entered the crater floor, filled with tourists on safari—people who had traveled to see nature up close. Some had come to see the formidable predators. Others hoped to glimpse the stouthearted black rhino before its numbers dwindled even more. Still others hoped to spot a dazzling herd of zebra stripes, a lanky cheetah with its speed, or a secretive leopard sprawled in the crook of an acacia tree. Mari couldn't choose which she loved best. She had come to see them all.

One by one, her teammates came and sat next to her. It was hard to believe they had not known one another a month before, but amazing to think about all that they had accomplished. Later, there would be a chance to call home, enjoy a victory dinner, and say their inevitably awkward good-byes. But for now, they all sat together and were filled with awe. From the Amazon to the Great Barrier Reef, to the Arctic Ocean and now here in the African savanna, they had covered a lot of ground during this race. They had found adventure and hidden strengths and friendship. But most of all, they had shared the wonder of seeing so much of the wild, wild world. Mari hoped that somehow, they might get to see even more.

# JOIN THE RACE!

It's an incredible adventure through the animal kingdom, as kids zip-line, kayak, and scuba dive their way to the finish line! Packed with cool facts about amazing creatures, dangerous habitats, and more!